the Shoe People

SERGEANT MAJOR

by James Driscoll
Illustrated by Rob Lee

Storm Publishing

Sergeant Major served most of his life as an army officer. He is a first class soldier.

He always seems to shout when he speaks. In fact, he can't speak quietly like you or me. He spent such a long time shouting orders to soldiers in the army that shouting became a habit.

His friends in Shoe Street know that he doesn't mean to shout. It just happens.

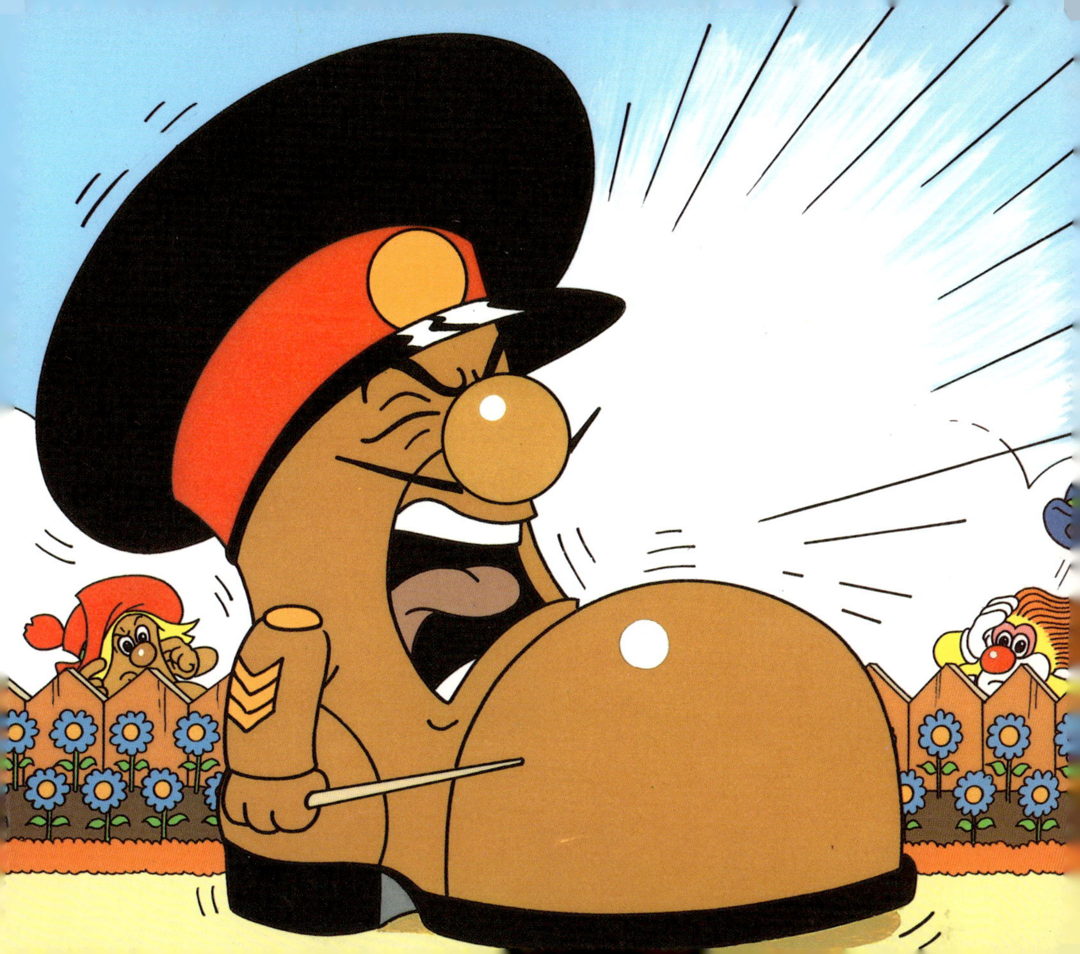

Sergeant Major lives in a very interesting house. It looks just like an army hut, the type you would see at an army barracks.

There is a flagpole at the side of his house from which flies a brightly coloured flag.

Sergeant Major calls his house Drill Hall.

DRILL HALL

Sergeant Major is a stickler for smartness.

He always wants everyone to look their best and he makes sure that he looks very smart at all times. The badge on Sergeant Major's hat is so highly polished that you can see your face in it. He spends hours and hours polishing it.

"CAN'T BEAT BEING SPICK AND SPAN!" he often says in his loud voice.

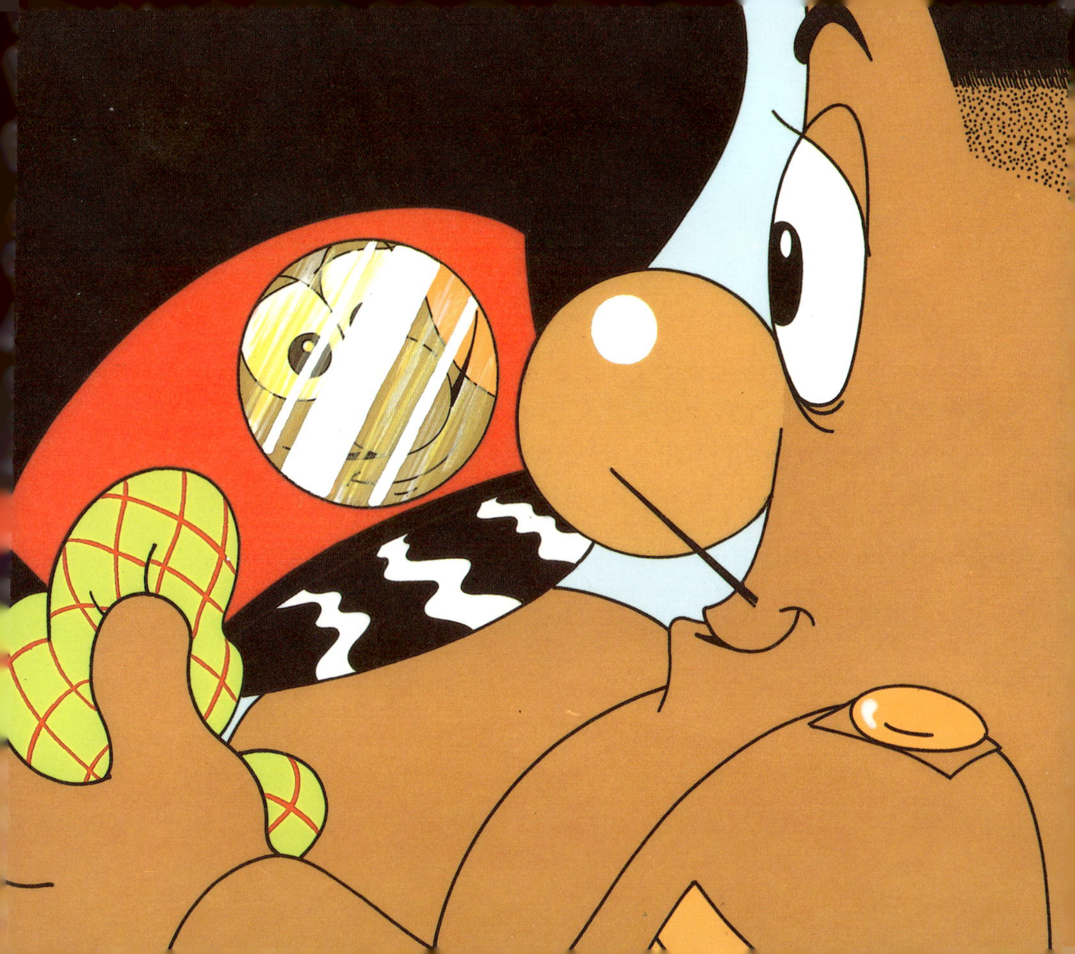

There is a large area at the back of Drill Hall which has been laid with paving slabs. Every morning Sergeant Major comes out of Drill Hall and stands to attention on the slabs.

He shouts in his loudest voice, "BY THE LEFT, QUICK MARCH!" and then starts marching up and down.

He thinks it is most important to march every day.

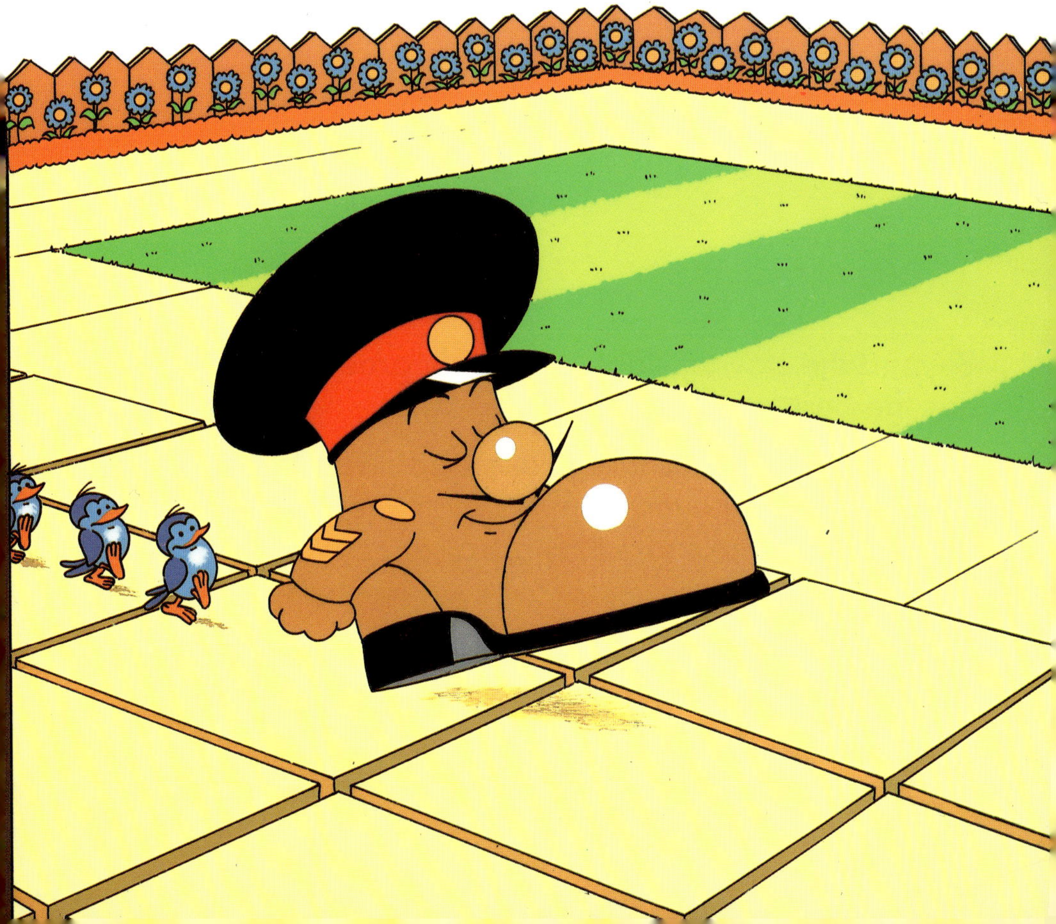

Beyond the paving slabs is a lovely green lawn. Drill Hall has the best kept lawn in Shoe Town.

Sergeant Major cuts it regularly and it has the straightest stripes you have ever seen. He even measures the stripes with a ruler to make sure thay are all exactly the same width.

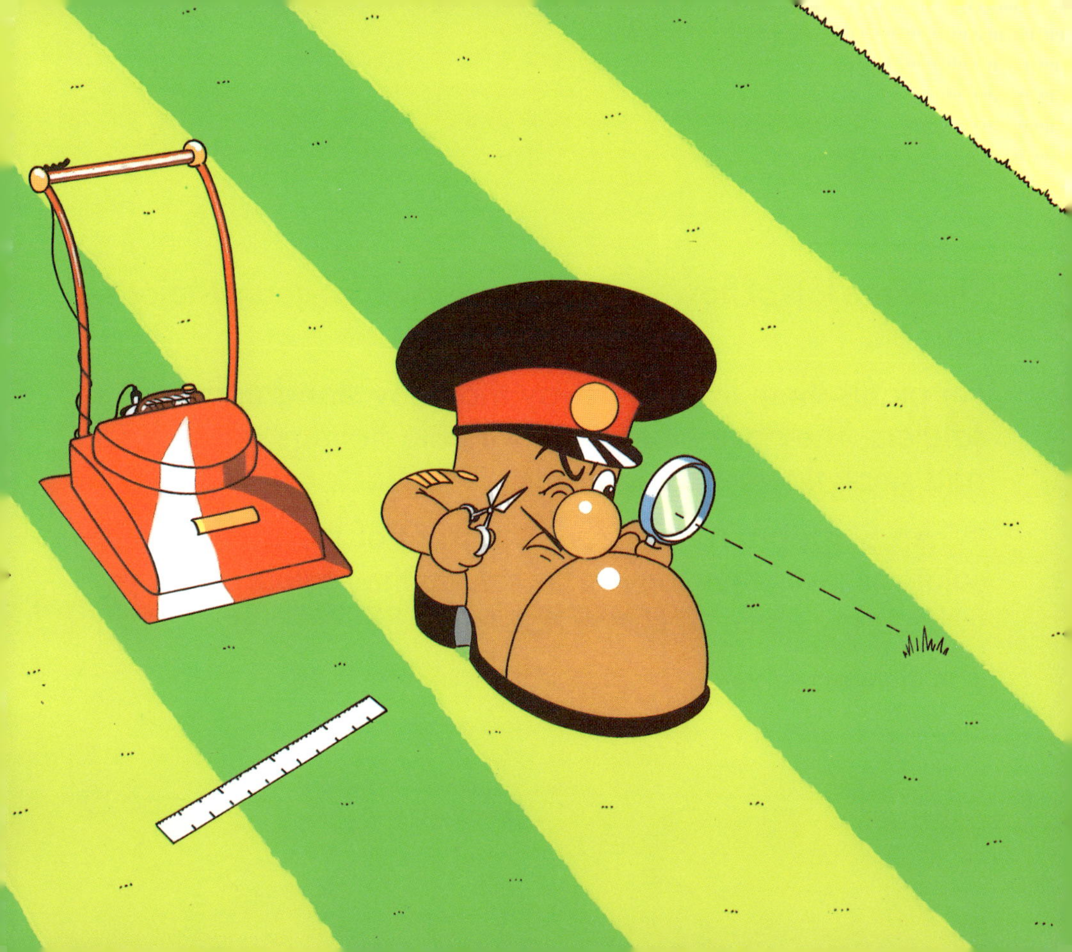

There are lots of flowers in the borders of Sergeant Major's garden.

He plants them in such a way that they stand upright like soldiers. They are all in rows with big flowers at the back and small flowers at the front.

When Sergeant Major stands in front of the flowers they salute him with their leaves. He returns their salute and says in his army voice, "FLOWERS! AT EASE!"

The flowers smile.

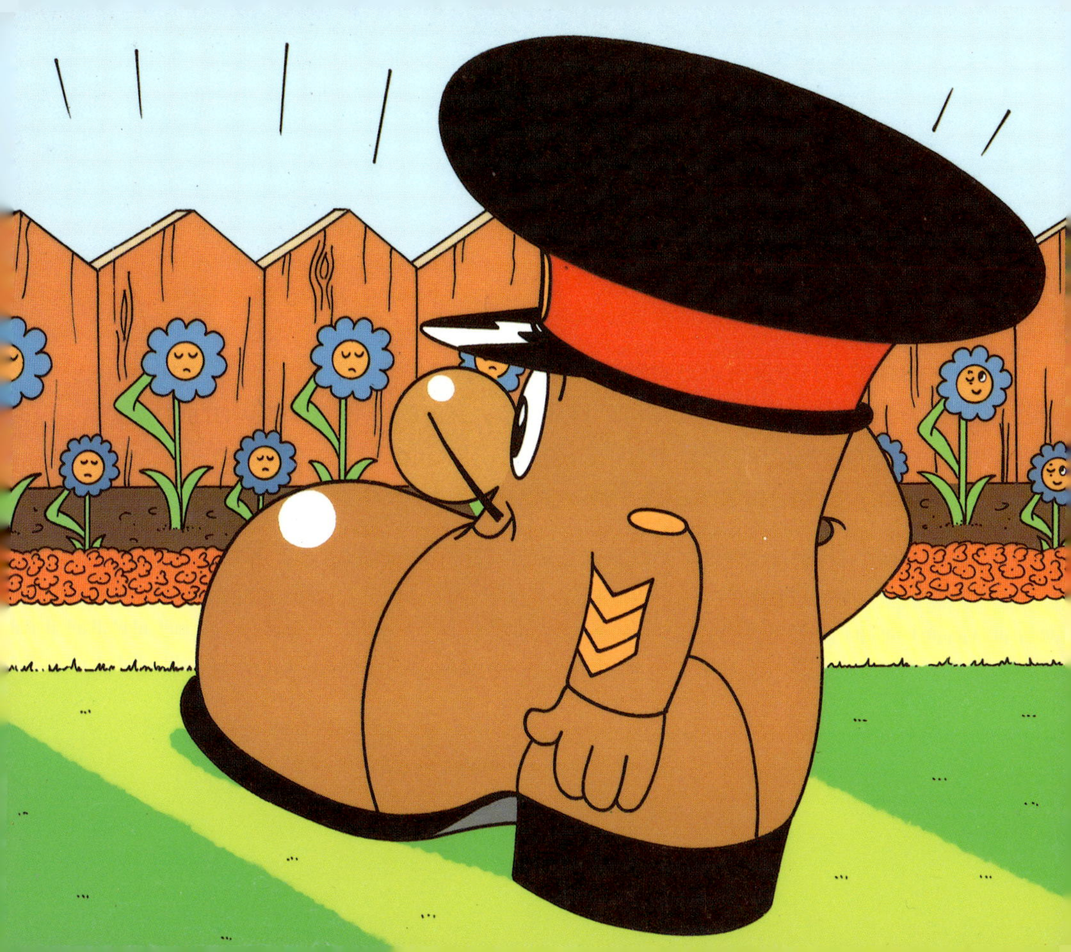

Sergeant Major lives next door to Trampy and this sometimes proves to be a problem. Trampy loves wild flowers and nature so much that he never cuts down anything in his garden. Trampy's wild flowers just grow and grow.

Some of them even grow over the fence into Sergeant Major's garden.

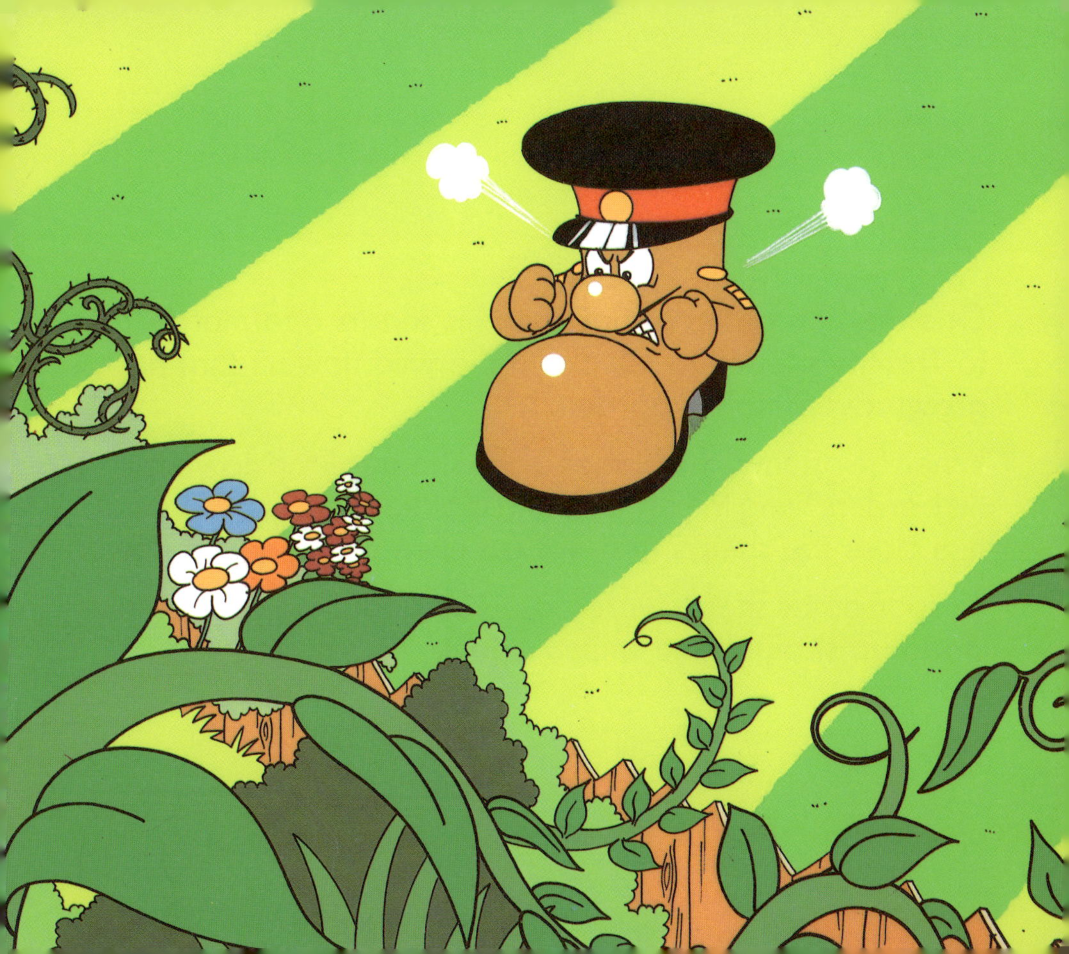

One day, Sergeant Major took his shears and marched up to Trampy's fence to cut down the wild flowers that had grown over into his garden.

When he opened the blades of the shears all the flowers in his borders hung their heads and looked very sad. This made him close the shears and not cut even a single wild flower.

As soon as the shears were closed Sergeant Major's flowers stood up straight and smiled again.

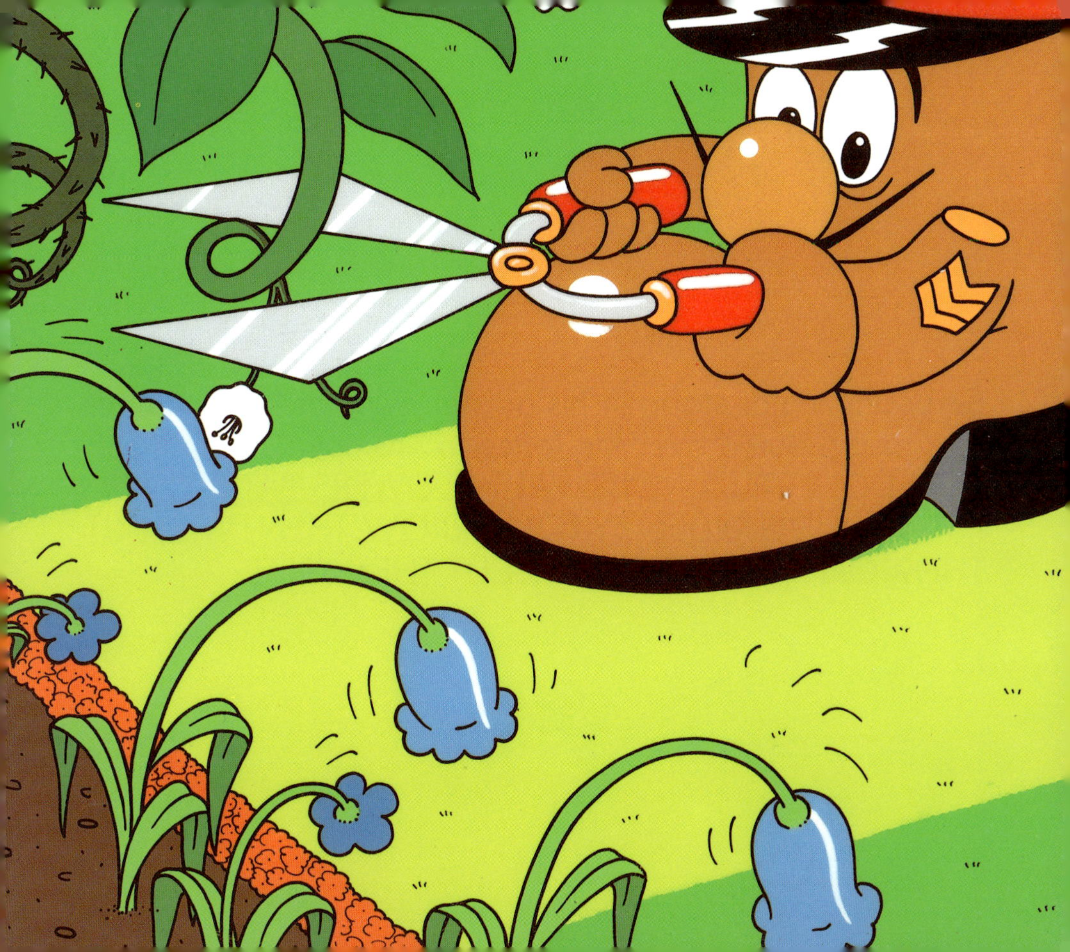

Sergeant Major stood in his garden with his hands on his hips and shouted over the fence to Trampy, "TRAMPY! IF YOU DON'T PULL YOUR WILD FLOWERS BACK OVER INTO YOUR GARDEN BY TOMORROW, THEN I WILL CUT THEM OFF. IS THAT CLEAR? CUT THEM OFF!".

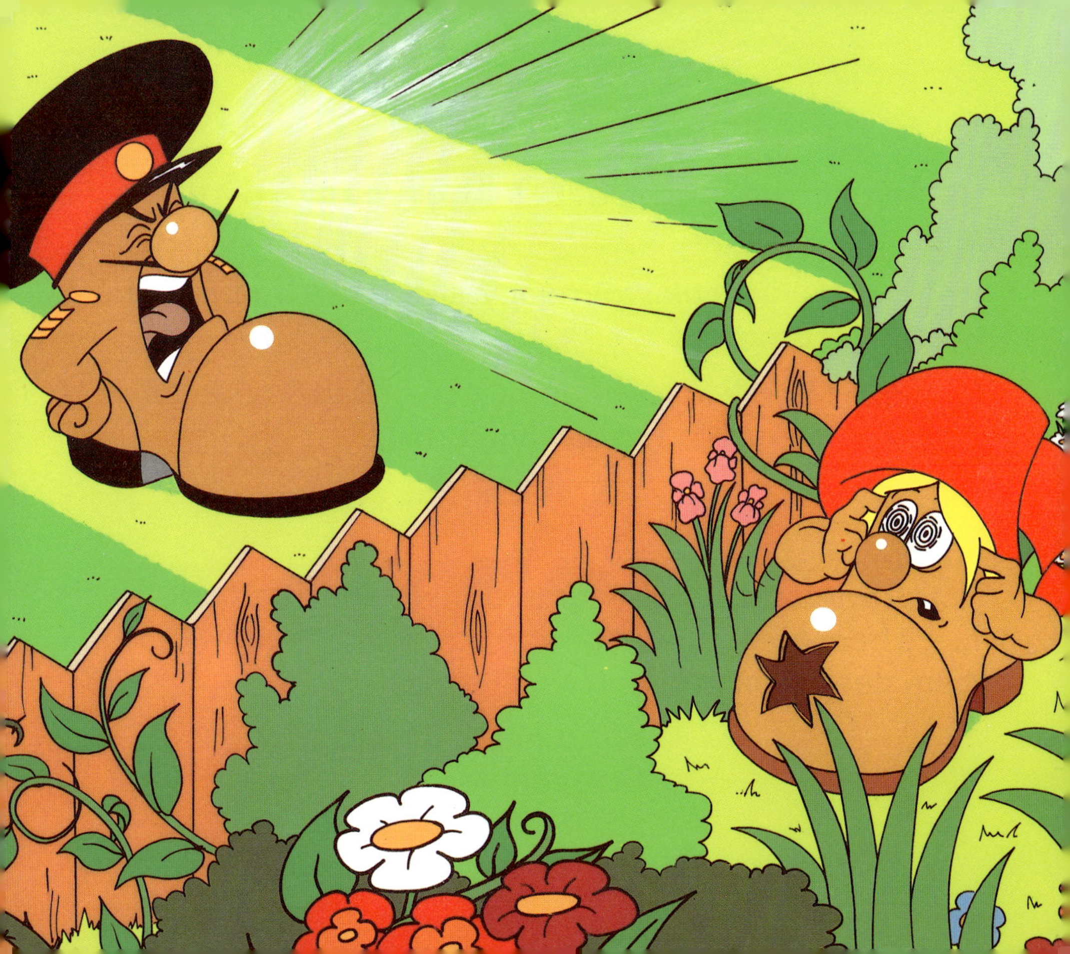

He then marched back inside Drill Hall and took out a pen and some paper.

He always writes notes to Trampy, just in case Trampy hasn't heard him properly.

Sergeant Major's note was not just an ordinary note, but an official army order. This is what it said:

ARMY ORDER

Trampy,
You are ordered to pull your wild flowers back through the fence from my garden at once. If you do not, then I will cut them down tomorrow.

Signed
Sergeant Major

When he had finished writing, he folded the order into the shape of a paper dart and sent it over the fence into Trampy's garden.

Sergeant Major always threatens to cut Trampy's flowers down.

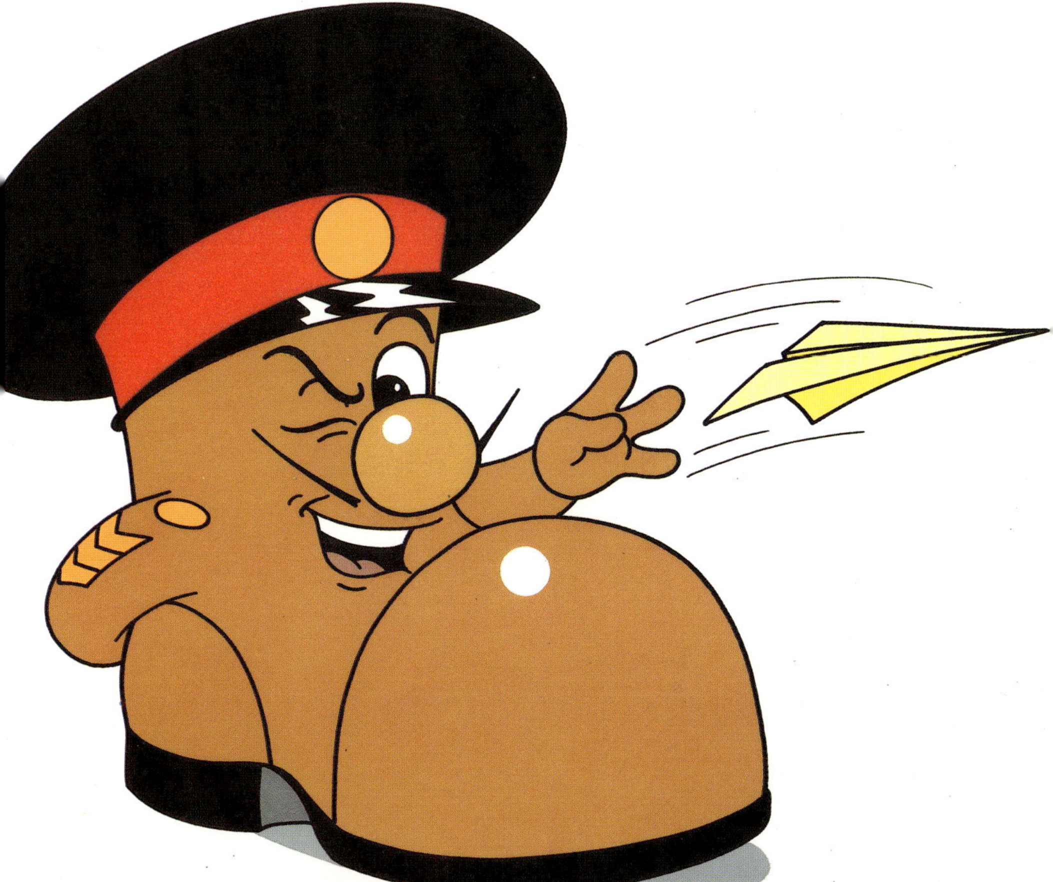

But he never does.